THE NEW LiBEARIAN

STORY BY Alison Donald

PICTURES BY Alex Willmore

CLARION BOOKS
Houghton Mifflin Harcourt
Boston New York

CLARION BOOKS
3 Park Avenue
New York, New York 10016

First published in Great Britain in 2016 by Maverick Arts Publishing,
Studio 3A, City Business Centre,
6 Brighton Road, Horsham, West Sussex RH13 5BB.

Published in the U.S. in 2018

Clarion Books is an imprint of Houghton Mifflin Harcourt Publishing Company.

www.hmhco.com

The illustrations were done in pencil and digital media.
The text was set in Century Gothic.

Library of Congress Cataloging-in-Publication Data
Names: Donald, Alison, author. | Willmore, Alex, illustrator. Title: The new liBEARian / story by Alison Donald ; pictures by Alex Willmore.
Description: New York : Clarion Books, 2017. | Summary: "When the children discover a bear at the librarian's desk at story time,
they think he's the new librarian. He's not!"— Provided by publisher. Identifiers: LCCN 2016033906 | ISBN 9780544973657 (hardcover)
Subjects: | CYAC: Storytelling—Fiction. | Bears—Fiction. | Libraries—Fiction. | Librarians—Fiction. Classification: LCC PZ7.7.D637 Ne 2017 | DDC [E]—dc23
LC record available at https://lccn.loc.gov/2016033906

Manufactured in China
SCP 10 9 8 7 6 5 4 3 2 1
4500673601

For Alastair, Kenzie, Gemma,
and Alexander, with whom life
is one big adventure!—A.D.
For Dara—A.W.

It was almost story time.
The children were ready.

Dee couldn't wait.

"Isn't it time?" she asked.

But no one answered.

Jack looked around. "Our librarian isn't here," he said.

"Maybe she's just late," said Dee.

"Ms. Merryweather is never late," said Kenzie.

"Then she's missing!" said Dee. "Let's go find her!"

"Look! A clue! Footprints," said Dee.

"They aren't grownup footprints," said Jack.

"They aren't kid footprints," said Alex.

Dee looked closer.

"They're paw prints," she declared.

They followed the paw prints among the bookshelves,

through a galaxy, into an ocean, and down a runway . . .

and spotted more clues.

101
RECIPES
FOR
HONEY

"The librarian's desk feels sticky," said Jack.

"These books are shredded and torn," said Dee.

And then they looked up and saw . . .

a new librarian!

"You're not our librarian.

Where's Ms. Merryweather?" Dee asked.

The new librarian shrugged.

"Will you read us a story?"

Dee asked.

The new librarian nodded.

"Hurray!" cried the children.

"A princess story?"

"A pirate story?"

"A book about dragons?"

The new librarian looked bored.

"How about something different?"
Gemma suggested.

"Something exciting,"
said Jameson.

"Something we aren't
allowed to read," said Tom.

"Could you read us a scary story?" asked Dee.
The new librarian's ears perked up.
He grabbed a book . . .

about **bears!**

He opened the book and **ROARED!!!**

"EEEEE!" the children screamed.

He **GROWLED**

and **STOMPED**

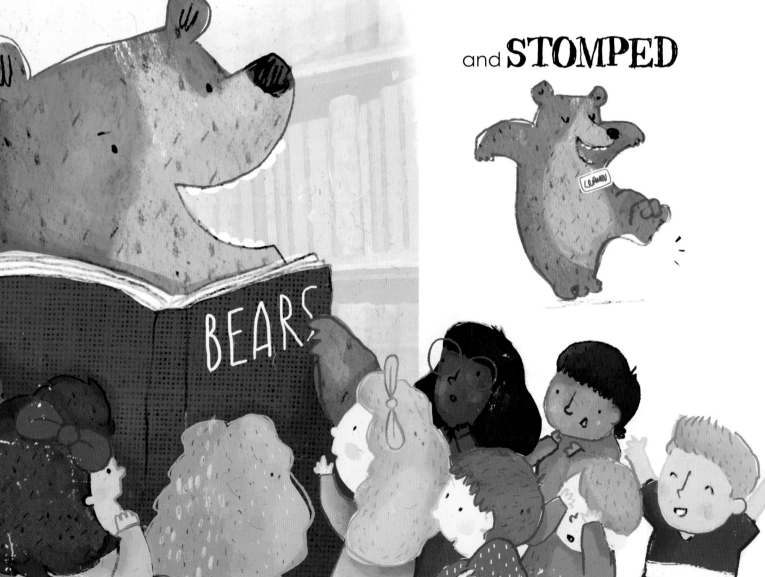

and **ROARED** some more.

BEAR

EARS

The children loved it.

"Read it again!" they cried.

"Someone's coming," said Dee.

It was the missing Ms. Merryweather. "Sorry I'm late," she said.

"A volcano erupted in the Ancient History section, and there

was hot lava everywhere. But it's all cleared up now."

Ms. Merryweather opened her book.

"Today's story is 'Goldilocks and the Three Bears.'"

"Ooh, we love bear stories!" Dee exclaimed.

"Once upon a time, there were three bears: Papa Bear, Mama Bear, and Baby—oh!"

"Where's Baby Bear?" the children cried.

"I know you're hiding, Baby Bear," said Ms. Merryweather.

"It's time to come out now."

The new librarian shuffled over sheepishly.

"Baby Bear, my dear, you're late for story time too,"

said Ms. Merryweather.

The children waved goodbye as Baby Bear
stepped back into his story.

"Now, let's start again,"
said Ms. Merryweather.

". . . and Baby Bear. A little girl came
to their house—

"Wait! Where's Goldilocks?"